MW00880672

SKATEBOARD POWER

by Jonny Zucker

illustrated by
Paul Savage

Librarian Reviewer
Joanne Bongaarts
Educational Consultant
MS in Library Media Education, Minnesota State University, Mankato, MN
Teacher and Media Specialist with Edina Public Schools, MN, 1993–2000

Reading Consultant
Elizabeth Stedem
Educator/Consultant, Colorado Springs, CO
MA in Elementary Education, University of Denver, CO

STONE ARCH BOOKS
Minneapolis   San Diego

First published in the United States in 2006
by Stone Arch Books,
151 Good Counsel Drive, P.O. Box 669,
Mankato, Minnesota 56002.
www.stonearchbooks.com

Originally published in Great Britain in 2005
by Badger Publishing Ltd.

Library of Congress Cataloging-in-Publication Data
Zucker, Jonny.
    Skateboard Power / by Jonny Zucker; illustrated by Paul Savage.
    p. cm.
    "Keystone Books."
    Summary: As Nick is preparing for a big skateboarding competition, a
bully tries to prevent him from entering, but Nick gets help from an unlikely
source.
    ISBN-13: 978-1-59889-007-5 (hardcover)
    ISBN-10: 1-59889-007-7 (hardcover)
    [1. Skateboarding—Fiction. 2. Bullies—Fiction. 3. Contests—Fiction.]
I. Savage, Paul, 1971– ill. II. Title.
PZ7.Z77925Ska 2006
[Fic]—dc22   2005026562

1 2 3 4 5 6 11 10 09 08 07 06

Printed in the United States of America

TABLE OF CONTENTS

Chapter 1

SKATEBOARD CITY

Nick Jones spun in the air and landed on the ground. He came to the skateboard park every day after school and on most weekends.

Today, the skateboard park was full of people trying out new tricks. Like him, they were getting ready for the skateboard competition. It was only two weeks away.

Nick got off his board and felt a hand on his shoulder. It was Dan Abbot, the neighborhood bully.

"I've been watching you," said Dan. "You're good."

Nick smiled. "Thanks."

But Dan wasn't smiling.

"You're too good," Dan said. "I want you to stay away from the park and forget about the competition. I'm going to win. If you turn up, people might think you're better than me."

"Forget it. I'm going to compete," said Nick.

Dan pushed Nick against a wall.

"I mean it," Dan said. "I don't want to see you here again!"

Chapter 2

THINK ABOUT IT

Nick lay in his bed that night, thinking about Dan. Maybe he should listen to Dan. Maybe he should stay away from the park and forget about the competition. He didn't want to get in a fight.

Nick got up and walked across the room. His skateboard was on the floor. He picked it up and looked at it. It was black and red with lots of stickers.

Nick stood in front of his mirror, holding the board and thinking about what Dan had said.

Nick was good, and he knew it.

Finally, he made up his mind. He would continue going to the park, and he would enter the competition.

Chapter 3

A HELPFUL CALL

The next day after school, Nick went to the skateboard park. He looked around. There was no sign of Dan. He walked to the top of one of the ramps and flew down it.

An hour later, Nick was finished. He'd done some good jumps and turns. A few of the other kids nodded at him as he left the park.

It was getting dark as he headed home. He turned a corner, and there was someone blocking his way.

It was Dan.

"I told you to stay away from the park," said Dan.

"I know what you said," replied Nick, "but I don't care. I'm going to go there whenever I want, and you can't stop me."

Dan moved a step closer and grabbed Nick's shirt. "I can stop you, and I *will* stop you."

At that moment, they heard a voice. "Leave him alone, Abbot."

Dan looked around.

It was Ted Smith.

Ted was in the seventh grade. Other kids called him Weirdo because he hung out after school in the shop class, working on designs and building stuff.

"I told you to leave him alone," Ted repeated.

"Okay, Weirdo," said Dan, letting go of Nick's shirt. "I'll leave you two alone, but Nick, you better not go to the park again."

Dan walked off.

Nick turned around to thank Ted, but Ted was gone.

Chapter 4

BUSTED BOARD

The next day after school, Nick went to get his skateboard. He left it in his locker.

When he got to the lockers, he stopped. His locker door was open. His skateboard was on the floor — in three pieces. Someone had smashed it.

There was no way he could fix it.

With no board, there was no point in going to the skateboard park. He'd have to forget the competition, too.

Dan would get his way.

As Nick walked out of the school, he saw Dan sitting in his older brother's beat-up sports car.

"Where's your skateboard?" Dan shouted out of the window.

"Get lost," Nick yelled back.

"Loser!" called Dan.

Then Dan and his brother zoomed off.

Chapter 5

SIMPLY THE BEST

In shop class the next morning, Ted sat in the back of the room making a metal tower.

As Nick walked in, he saw Dan and sat down next to him.

"You smashed my board," said Nick.

"Get lost," Dan said. "Why don't you go and sit with Weirdo?"

"I know it was you," said Nick.

"Prove it!"

As they argued, the shop teacher, Mr. Best, was starting class.

"You know you did it," said Nick.

Dan looked at him. "I don't know what you're talking about."

"I don't even know which locker is yours," Dan added.

"Who said anything about lockers?" Nick asked.

"What's going on there?" asked Mr. Best. "Stop talking."

But Nick wasn't listening. He was yelling at Dan.

"You owe me, Abbot!" he screamed.

Mr. Best shouted across the room. "Nick Jones, I told you to stop talking! You've got detention after school!"

"Tough luck," smiled Dan.

Chapter 6

RFTER-SCHOOL HASSLE

Nick hated detention. He had
to stay an extra hour after school.
It meant getting to the skateboard
park late.

But that didn't matter anymore. His
board was broken. He'd never be able
to prove Dan broke it.

Nick couldn't enter the competition.

"Trouble with Abbot again?" a voice asked from behind Nick.

Nick looked around. It was Ted.

Nick nodded. "Thanks for your help the other day."

"Forget it," said Ted.

Mr. Best called to Nick. "You're talking again, Nick. If you don't keep quiet, you'll get another detention."

Nick opened his math book.

Chapter 7

SHOP CLASS

The next day, Dan saw Nick staying after school. "Detention again?" Dan laughed at Nick.

Nick didn't say anything. Every day that week, he headed to the shop after his last class.

On Friday, Nick was getting his bike from the bike shed. Dan was with his older brother.

Dan walked over to Nick.

"Things don't look too good for you," Dan said with a smile. "First your board gets smashed, and now you've got detention every day."

Nick turned his back on Dan.

Dan laughed and walked back over to his brother.

But Nick didn't look angry. He smiled as he walked away.

Chapter 8

JUSTICE

The day of the competition, kids started showing up at the park around 2:00 in the afternoon. Dan was there, doing tricks and showing off.

The man running the competition arrived. He started talking about the rules. Just then, Dan saw Nick walking up to the gate of the park.

Nick was carrying a big blue bag, and Ted Smith was with him.

Dan pushed his way to the gate and stood in Nick's way.

"What are you doing here? And why is Weirdo with you?" Dan asked.

"You know I've been staying after school, don't you?" Nick asked.

"It's always good to see someone else getting detention," grinned Dan.

Nick laughed. "I was only in detention once — the day I shouted at you in Mr. Best's class. The other times, I went to shop class," explained Nick. "I was working with Ted."

"What are you talking about?" Dan asked.

Ted reached into the blue bag and pulled out a brand-new, silver skateboard.

Dan looked at it in shock.

"Where did you get that?" Dan wanted to know.

"We made it," replied Nick. "It's great, isn't it?"

Dan suddenly lunged at Ted, trying to grab the skateboard. Nick stepped between them, and Dan tripped over Nick's foot.

Dan fell and hit the ground hard.

"My knee!" he cried out in pain.

"You hurt?" Nick asked. "You probably won't be able to enter the competition now."

Dan tried to get up but couldn't. His knee hurt a lot. He pulled himself up onto a bench.

Chapter 9

THE CONTEST

Nick walked into the skateboard park. Ted stayed outside. A large group of kids turned around to look at Nick's new board. The man running the competition looked, too.

"Is that boy on the bench here for the competition?" the man asked Nick.

He was pointing at Dan, who was still sitting, rubbing his knee.

"Dan?" Nick asked, grinning at Ted. "I don't think he's up to it."

"What about you?" the man wanted to know.

Nick smiled and put his board down on the ramp.

"I'm ready!" he exclaimed.

ABOUT THE AUTHOR

As a kid, Jonny Zucker always wanted to be a writer. He often got in trouble for writing stories in school when he was supposed to be paying attention.

Jonny worked as a teacher and wrote books whenever he could. Today, he writes full-time and lives in London, England, with his wife and two kids.

ABOUT THE ILLUSTRATOR

Paul Savage works in a design studio, drawing pictures for advertising. He says illustrating books is "the best job." He's always been interested in illustrating books, and he loves reading. Paul also enjoys playing sports and running.

He lives in England with his wife and daughter, Amelia.

GLOSSARY

competition (kom-puh-TISH-uhn)—a situation in which two or more people are trying to win the same thing, such as a skateboarding contest

detention (di-TEN-shuhn)—a punishment in which a student has to stay after school

hassle (HASS-uhl)—a problem, such as a fight

justice (JUHSS-tiss)—fair treatment

lunge (LUHNJ)—to move forward quickly and suddenly

ramp (RAMP)—a slope used for performing skateboard jumps and tricks

DISCUSSION QUESTIONS

1. If Nick and Dan both competed in the skateboard competition, who do you think would win? Why?

2. When Dan threatens Nick outside the skateboard park, Ted steps in and defends Nick. Why does Ted do this? What does Ted have to gain by helping Nick?

3. What happens after the story ends? Does Nick win the competition? How would that make Dan feel?

WRITING PROMPTS

1. Dan wanted Nick to quit the skateboard competition, so he would have a better chance at winning. But even if he competed against Nick, Dan still could have won. Write about how Dan would feel if he had won the skateboard competition fair and square. Would he feel differently than if he had won it by cheating?

2. Write what you would do if you saw a bully picking on someone. Would you help like Ted did? Why or why not?

3. Have you ever bullied someone in order to get your own way? Or have you ever been bullied? Write about your experience.

ALSO BY JONNY ZUCKER

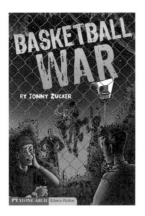

Basketball War
1-59889-009-3

Jim and Ali are determined to beat the Langham Jets in the upcoming basketball championship. But the boys learn that there's something strange about their rival's new coach.

Steel Eyes
1-59889-019-0

Emma Stone is the new girl in school. Why does she always wear sunglasses? Gail and Tanya are determined to find out, but Emma's cold stare is more than they bargained for.

OTHER BOOKS IN THIS SET

Nervous
Tony Norman
1-59889-018-2

It's time for the Dream Stars Talent Show. The cool kids think their band Elite is a sure win. But what happens when a couple of nerds decide to start up their own band called Nervous?

Webcam Scam
by J. Powell

1-59889-011-5

Carl's family is thrilled when they are chosen for a reality Web show. But Carl has his doubts. When it seems that there is more to it than meets the eye, Carl has to act.

Internet Sites

Do you want to know more about subjects related to this book? Or are you interested in learning about other topics? Then check out FactHound, a fun, easy way to find Internet sites.

Our investigative staff has already sniffed out great sites for you!

Here's how to use FactHound:

1. Visit *www.facthound.com*

2. Select your grade level.

3. To learn more about subjects related to this book, type in the book's ISBN number: **1598890077**.

4. Click the **Fetch It** button.

FactHound will fetch the best Internet sites for you!